This book belongs to:

Draw your picture here

Write your name here

D0681260

With special thanks to Lil Chase

Ellie's Magical Bakery: PERFECT PIE FOR A PERFECT PET
A RED FOX BOOK 978 1 782 95267 1

First published in Great Britain by Red Fox,
an imprint of Random House Children's Publishers UK
A Random House Group Company

This edition published 2014

1 3 5 7 9 10 8 6 4 2

The Random House Group Limited supports the Forest Stewardship Council® (FSC®), the
leading international forest-certification organisation. Our books carrying the FSC label are
printed on FSC®-certified paper. FSC is the only forest-certification scheme supported by the
leading environmental organisations, including Greenpeace. Our paper procurement policy
can be found at www.randomhouse.co.uk/environment

MIX
Paper from
responsible sources
FSC® C016897

Red Fox Books are published by Random House Children's Publishers UK,
61–63 Uxbridge Road, London W5 5SA

www.**randomhousechildrens**.co.uk
www.**totallyrandombooks**.co.uk
www.**randomhouse**.co.uk

Addresses for companies within The Random House Group Limited
can be found at: www.randomhouse.co.uk/offices.htm

THE RANDOM HOUSE GROUP Limited Reg. No. 954009

A CIP catalogue record for this book is available from the British Library.

Printed and bound in Great Britain by CPI Group (UK) Ltd, Croydon CR0 4YY

Ellie's Magical Bakery

Perfect Pie for a Perfect Pet

ELLIE SIMMONDS

Illustrated by Kimberley Scott

RED FOX

Village Hall

POST OFFICE

SUPERMARKET

...yton High Street

SCRUDGES

Scrudges Bakery

GREYTON

Chapter 1

"Goodbye." Ellie waved at Mr Amrit and his wife. "Come back tomorrow!"

"Oh, we will!" Mr and Mrs Amrit waved back. "And thank you for another lovely cake!" They walked away from Ellie's Magical Bakery, the smallest shop on Greyton High Street. The shop had an open counter at the front so that Ellie could serve people passing by.

She pulled down the shutters. It was

4.30 p.m.: time to close.

"Phew!" Ellie sighed. "Another busy day!" But she was happy. The bakery had only been open for a few weeks and it already had plenty of regular customers. She smiled at Whisk, her ginger cat, who was playing on the counter.

"The day's not quite over yet," said Ellie's best friend, Basil. He was putting on his roller skates. "We still have the deliveries to do."

"And I want to see what new recipes there are in my recipe book," said Ellie.

She pulled a stool over to the book shelf and stood on it so that she could reach. She was grabbing the only book she ever needed to use – her *magical* recipe book. It was filled with amazing recipes for all occasions! When Ellie followed them, somehow her wishes came true . . . Like when she'd baked the *Best cake for a best friend*, which had helped her find her best

friend, Basil.

But the magical recipes weren't the only special thing about her book . . .

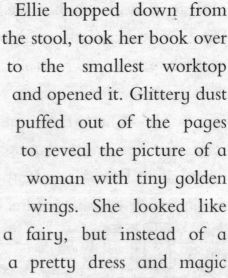

Ellie hopped down from the stool, took her book over to the smallest worktop and opened it. Glittery dust puffed out of the pages to reveal the picture of a woman with tiny golden wings. She looked like a fairy, but instead of a crown, a pretty dress and magic wand, she had a chef's hat, a white apron and a wooden spoon!

Ellie whispered, "Victoria Sponge . . . ?" As if just saying the words worked some sort of spell, the little baker began to peel out of the book. She flew up into the air, leaving a trail of glitter behind her.

"Good afternoon, Ellie." Victoria Sponge twirled around Ellie's head, making her long brown hair fly up. The little baker cast her eye about the room: there was flour on the worktops, cake tins to be washed, and the floor needed a mop. "What a day we've had!"

"It's been so busy," Ellie agreed.

"And we still have three cakes to deliver," said Basil.

"Not to mention the tidying up we have to do," Ellie added.

"Miaow." Whisk wanted to join in.

Victoria Sponge popped on a pair of rubber gloves. "I can help you with the tidying."

"Thank you." Ellie went over to the sink and turned on the taps. "That would be—" But when she looked round again, the floor of the bakery was clean and shiny. "Oh!"

She went back to the washing-up, but the cake tins were already sparkling on the drying rack. "Oh!" she said again.

"Wowweee," said Basil.

Victoria Sponge often used magic, but it still amazed Ellie and Basil.

Since the bakery had opened, Ellie, Basil, Victoria Sponge and Whisk had worked out a routine: every morning Victoria Sponge helped Ellie in the kitchen, making cakes, cookies, biscuits, pies and pastries, while Basil sold the cakes, cookies and biscuits, pies and pastries to the customers in the shop.

7

And when the shop closed at the end of the day, Ellie prepared for the next day's baking. She always checked her magical recipe book for interesting recipes to try! Victoria Sponge cleaned up – mostly by magic. And Basil filled boxes from the pyramid-shaped stack with cakes, ready to be delivered. Even Whisk lent a paw, sticking stickers onto the boxes. It was a lot of hard work, but none of them minded – running Ellie's Magical Bakery was so much fun!

The last job of the day was making deliveries.

"I'll wait here while you deliver the cakes," said Victoria Sponge.

Ellie and Basil carefully placed the three cake boxes into the bakery's little cart. Basil smoothed down his T-shirt — today it had a lizard on it — and then they set off. Basil whizzed along on his roller skates, and he and Ellie took it in turns to pull the cart behind them. It got heavier when Whisk jumped in, though.

"Lazy cat," said Ellie with a chuckle.

Whisk just cleaned his whiskers with his paws.

They wheeled the cart up the high street and turned off into a little side road.

"What's the number of the house?" Basil asked Ellie.

She was about to check her piece of paper, but then she saw a house with a bunch of bright blue balloons tied to the gate. "There!" she pointed.

As they got closer, Ellie could see that the balloons read:

10

Happy Birthday Abdul – the same message she had iced onto the cake.

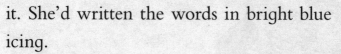

Ellie had baked Abdul a vanilla sponge, and the creamy icing had blueberries whipped into it. She'd written the words in bright blue icing.

Ellie pulled the cart over to the gate as Basil skated along beside her.

Suddenly Whisk stood up in the cart, his fur standing on end.

As soon as Ellie heard a *"Yip, yip, yip!"* from the garden, she understood why.

Basil looked over the fence and laughed. "Don't worry, Whisk," he said. "It's only a tiny puppy."

Ellie peered over too. The puppy was very tiny indeed, with a black body and a brown nose, and a bright blue ribbon around his neck. "Hello, puppy," she said.

"Hello!" came a voice from up the path.

Ellie looked up to see a little boy in a bright blue T-shirt come running out of the house. "Hello!" he said again. "Don't be scared of my puppy – he's very playful but he is also very good." The boy picked up his puppy, which gave him a lick on the cheek.

Ellie opened the gate and patted the little dog on the head. He had a very long body, but very short legs.

Ellie had short legs too – she had a condition called

Achondroplasia, which meant that her arms and her legs were shorter than most people's. "What kind of dog is he?" she asked.

"He's a sausage dog," said the boy.

Basil skated closer so he could give the puppy a stroke. "What's his name?"

"He doesn't have a name yet," the boy told them. "I got him for my birthday, which is today!"

"Then you must be Abdul!" Ellie handed over the cake. "Happy birthday, Abdul!" she cried. "I'm Ellie. This is Basil. And this is my cat, Whisk. We're from Ellie's Magical Bakery."

Whisk bobbed his head and said, "Miaow," which was his way of saying hello.

"Thank you," Abdul replied. He looked at the puppy he held in one hand and the cake he held in the other. "This is going to be the best birthday ever!"

Ellie and Basil chuckled as they pulled the cart away.

"If you think of a good name for my new dog, please let me know," Abdul called as they left.

"We will." Ellie began thinking hard.

It would be very difficult to come up with the perfect name for Abdul's perfect pet.

Chapter 2

Ellie was tired as she pushed open the door to Scrudge's Bakery a little later. The first thing that hit her was the smell – sour milk and open bins. *Revolting, as usual*, she thought.

"Hello, Aunt, hello, Uncle," she called.

Ellie lived in the flat above this bakery with her aunt and uncle, and her cousin Colin – the Scrudge family. Her dad used

to own this bakery, but it was a much nicer place when he ran it. He had died three years ago. She remembered his ginger beard, round cheeks and silly deep chuckle. Whenever she thought about him she was surrounded by the aroma of freshly baked cakes. Mr and Mrs Scrudge only made horrible cakes; they sold mouldy buns and the bakery always smelled awful.

Her aunt was sitting on a chair behind the counter. She was too rude to say hello, but she looked at Ellie and her cat as if they were a rather nasty surprise.

Ellie's uncle came out of the kitchen. He was the size of a garden shed and his face was covered in black, spiky stubble which had bits of food in it. *Yuck!*

"Oh, it's *you*," he said, scowling at Ellie and Whisk. "I thought it might be someone good, like a customer."

Now that *was rude*, thought Ellie.

She was just about to say so, when suddenly Mrs Scrudge sat up straight and forced a smile onto her face. "Customer!" she screeched, and pointed at the door.

Ellie turned to see a man with a friendly smile come in. She'd met most people in Greyton, but she'd never seen this man before.

"Hello," she said. "Are you new to the village?"

"I'm not from here," the man replied, taking off his hat. "But I heard about a delightful bakery in Greyton, so I thought I would come and try it out."

Ellie blushed. She was pretty sure he wasn't talking about Scrudge's Bakery, and there was only one other bakery in Greyton – hers!

"Hello, sir." Mrs Scrudge batted her

20

eyelashes. "Do buy something from our delightful shop."

"Yes, that would be . . ." The man looked around at the shelves, but his smile slowly faded as he caught sight of the mould on every cake. He stepped forward, picked up a bun and grimaced, dropping it on his foot. He yelped. "Ow! That was rock hard."

"Er . . . yes," said Mrs Scrudge, her eyelashes moving so fast now that Ellie wondered if she had flour on them. "It's a rock cake!"

21

Ellie rolled her eyes. She'd made rock cakes before and they weren't supposed to be *that* hard.

Mr Scrudge came out of the kitchen and put his fists up. "You dropped that cake," he growled, "so now you've got to buy it. It's the law."

The man put his hat on and scowled right back at Mr Scrudge. "No, I do not," he said, and stormed out of the shop.

Ellie turned to her aunt and uncle. "Maybe if you made tasty cakes, then

22

people would come from miles around to buy them. Nobody wants rock cakes made from actual rocks!"

Mrs Scrudge tutted. "Nice rock cakes take too much effort. Our ones are easier by far."

"And cheaper," added Mr Scrudge, brushing the dandruff off his shoulder and into a tin marked SUGAR.

Yuck!

"I could help you if you like," said Ellie. She didn't want her aunt

and uncle to be enemies. She was sure that both bakeries could be popular if they both made really nice food.

But Mrs Scrudge just laughed, holding her belly.

"*You?*" spat Mr Scrudge. "You are too small and too stupid to help *us*. In fact, you're too small and too stupid to do anything. I bet your bakery is rubbish!"

Ellie might have been shorter than everyone else, but she wasn't stupid. "My bakery isn't rubbish! I work really hard and the customers are always happy."

Mrs Scrudge narrowed her eyes at Ellie and muttered something. It sounded like,

"Your bakery isn't rubbish? We'll see about that."

"Pardon?" asked Ellie.

"Nothing," replied Mrs Scrudge. She sounded almost nice for a change.

Ellie went upstairs to her bedroom with Whisk. "We're going to have to keep an eye on the Scrudges. I have a feeling they're up to something," she told him.

Whisk miaowed in agreement.

Chapter 3

Ping!

Ellie's cash register rang as it opened again and Basil put some money inside. It was still early in the morning, but Ellie's Magical Bakery had already served so many customers that she'd come to help Basil in the shop.

The shop till was always ringing these

days. But Ellie was so busy baking she didn't have time to spend the money she made!

"Wowweee," said Basil as he looked in the till drawer and saw the notes there. "What are you going to do with all this?" he asked.

Ellie shook her head. "I have no idea!" She took a deep breath and straightened her chef's hat. "Come on — we've got loads of cakes to make today!"

They headed into the bakery kitchen, where

Victoria Sponge was setting out their ingredients for the day.

"Yes, let's get started," she said, waving her wooden spoon.

As usual, Victoria Sponge helped Ellie with the cakes, while Basil kept an eye out for customers in the shop. They worked happily together, trying out some new recipes from the magical book – *Biscuits for breakfast*, *Fudge cake for Fridays* – Ellie even found a recipe for rock cakes and baked a batch of those. They were delicious – very different to the rock cakes in Scrudge's Bakery! Basil found time to

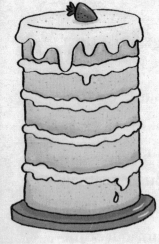

make his favourite treats – doughnuts with chocolate sprinkles. Victoria Sponge made her special cake: a gigantic five-layer Victoria sponge cake, which was ten times her size.

It was mid-morning when Ellie heard a whimpering noise coming from the street.

"What's that?" she wondered.

"What's *what*?" Basil asked.

Whisk stood by the door and miaowed. Ellie raced out to the front of the shop.

Abdul was standing just outside in a

bright blue jumper, a pile of papers in his hand. He was crying.

"Abdul! What's the matter?" asked Ellie.

"It's my new puppy." Abdul sniffed. "He's gone missing!"

He handed Ellie one of the pieces of paper. They were flyers that said *LOST PUPPY!* in big letters, and had a picture of Abdul hugging his pet and a telephone number in case anyone had seen the little dog.

"Oh dear!" Ellie brought Abdul inside and sat him down. Whisk jumped up onto his lap.

"What happened?" asked Basil as he

LOST
PUPPY

If anyone has seen
my puppy please call
0720-514-3355

joined them. Victoria Sponge had hidden herself in the kitchen — she wanted to remain a secret, so she only ever allowed Ellie, Basil and Whisk to see her.

Adbul sniffed back his tears, which made Whisk wobble a little. "My puppy is a perfect pet, but he's very playful."

Ellie remembered just how playful the little dog had been when they saw him yesterday.

"I couldn't find him anywhere this morning. Then I noticed

that the front gate was open!"

Ellie gasped. "He must have escaped!"

In the kitchen, she heard Victoria Sponge gasp too. The little baker was listening in.

"I tried to call out for him, but I couldn't . . ." said Abdul, his eyes filling with tears again.

"Why not?" Basil was frowning as deeply as the owl on his T-shirt.

"He doesn't have a name yet!" Abdul told him.

Ellie frowned too. She felt so sad for Abdul – she would be very worried if Whisk ever went missing. "I'm sure he'll turn up, but for now let's see if I can

find a recipe to help cheer you up," she suggested.

"Good idea, Ellie," said Basil.

Whisk miaowed. He agreed too.

Ellie got out her magical recipe book and placed it on the table in front of them. She flicked through the recipes, and saw:

A cake for a wet Wednesday
A bun for a summer barbecue
A muffin for when you're overexcited

. . . but no recipes to cheer up a person who'd lost their perfect pet.

Ellie reached the blank pages at the end of the book. She concentrated hard for a moment and made a wish that the perfect recipe would appear. She was hoping to find a recipe for a tasty treat that would make Abdul feel better . . . but nothing happened.

"I'm sorry, Abdul," she said. "I want to make something for you, but I can't find the right recipe."

"That's OK, Ellie." Abdul tried to smile. "Thanks anyway."

As he got up, Whisk jumped down off the boy's lap. "I'm going to carry on looking for my puppy." Abdul's head hung

low as he walked out of the door. "Please let me know if you see him," he said as he left.

"We will," promised Basil.

Ellie watched him go. She was worried about the little puppy and really wanted to lift Abdul's spirits. Why hadn't the magical book shown her a recipe to cheer him up? Normally, whenever Ellie had a problem, the book showed her the perfect recipe to help solve it. But this time it had given her nothing.

"Victoria Sponge!" she called.

The magical baker floated in from the kitchen, leaving a

trail of glitter behind her.

"Our new friend Abdul has lost his puppy," Basil told her.

Victoria Sponge pursed her lips. "Yes, I heard — that's very sad."

"And I couldn't find a recipe in the book to help cheer him up." Ellie was worried — what if the magic of the recipe book had stopped working? "Could the magic have gone?" she asked.

Victoria Sponge shook her head slowly. "It will always have an answer for you, Ellie. But I don't think anything will cheer

up Abdul except finding his missing puppy. Why don't you try the book again?"

It was worth a try – it was a *magical* book after all!

Ellie opened the book while Whisk wound round her legs for luck. She flicked through the pages, wondering how to find Abdul's puppy. But she saw only the same old recipes. "You see," she said, "there's nothing— What . . . ?" As she spoke, she saw a heading appear at

the end of the book:

A Perfect Pie for a Perfect Pet

Ellie gasped. "This wasn't here a minute ago!"

It wasn't a recipe to cheer Abdul up: it was even better – a recipe to help find his puppy. The book had come up with a solution after all!

"But recipes can only help you cook food – they can't find missing animals," Ellie pointed out.

"You're thinking of *normal* recipes . . ."

said Victoria Sponge with a wink. "These recipes are magical!

"What are we waiting for? Let's make the pie!" cried Basil.

But they *did* have to wait. The page below the heading was blank, so they didn't know what ingredients they needed. But all at once some words started to appear, wiggling across the page like worms.

"Wowweee!" said Basil.

It looked like this was going to be a very different sort of pie to the ones usually made in Ellie's Magical Bakery.

The first line of the recipe said they needed half a kilo of minced meat. A little handwritten note appeared beside it:

Frinton the butcher sells good quality meat.

Basil scratched his head. "What kind of pie has meat in it?"

Ellie laughed. "A *meat* pie!"

"Of course." Basil laughed too.

Whisk purred at the thought of a meat pie.

They waited for the next instruction of the recipe to appear . . . but the rest of

42

the page remained blank. "Are you *sure* the magic is still working?" Ellie asked Victoria Sponge, her hands on her hips.

Victoria Sponge picked up the book, put her ear to it and shook it. "Quite sure," she said, putting it down again and flashing a mischievous smile at them.

Ellie started to work out what else they would need to make a meat pie. "Maybe I should roll out some pastry," she wondered aloud.

But Victoria Sponge looked serious now. "You must follow the recipe precisely," she said.

"Go to the butcher's while I stay here and keep an eye on the food in the oven." Ellie had worked hard that morning and the last of her cakes were still baking.

Ellie put the magical recipe book in her bag, then hung a sign in the shop window that said:

CLOSED – SORRY!

She raced out, thanking Victoria Sponge as she went.

Whisk miaowed, which was his way of saying thank you too.

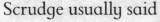

As soon as they'd gone through the door
— *thwack!* Ellie ran smack into something,
and fell backwards onto the pavement.

She pushed her hair out of her eyes and
looked up. "I'm sorry, I—" But she stopped
speaking as soon as she saw who it was.

Mr and Mrs Scrudge! Their son, Colin,
was with them too.

"Oh!" she said.

It was very strange to see the Scrudges
away from their horrible bakery Mr
Scrudge usually said

that the people of Greyton were too idiotic to spend time with.

"Hello, Auntie, Uncle, Colin," Ellie said. "I'm sorry, I wasn't looking where I was going." She winced, preparing to be shouted at.

"That's all right, dear," said Mrs Scrudge.

"These things happen," said Colin.

"Let me help you up," said Mr Scrudge, lifting her off the pavement as if she weighed nothing. "Are you OK?"

Ellie was too shocked to speak.

Basil was wide-eyed.

Whisk had his mouth hanging open.

Then Ellie noticed that Mr Scrudge had shaved off his stubble . . .

"She's fine." Basil pulled Ellie away from them.

"You three have a delightful day," said Mrs Scrudge, adding a merry wave as they left.

"Now *that*," said Ellie, when she finally found her voice, "was very strange indeed."

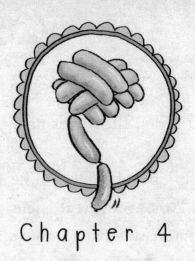

Chapter 4

A little bell tinkled when Ellie pushed open the door to the butcher's. She had been here a few times, whenever Mr Scrudge made her get fat to use in his shortbread instead of butter – *yuck!* Frinton's was an old-fashioned shop with sawdust on the floor and a counter where Mr Frinton, the butcher, sold cuts of meat. Behind the counter were jars of pickles and savoury

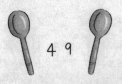

jams. But today there was no sign of Mr Frinton.

Whisk miaowed loudly – Ellie could tell he liked all the wonderful smells.

Mr Frinton suddenly stood up behind the counter, making Ellie jump. He was holding a stack of the waxed paper he used to wrap up the meat. The butcher sighed, and wiped his forehead with the back of his hand. "Sorry about that – I was just picking these up," he said. "How can I help you?"

"We're making a pie,"

Ellie told him, "and we need half a kilo of your finest minced meat, please."

"Coming right up!"

While he weighed out their order, Ellie looked around the shop and saw that it was quite messy — some jars of chutney had been knocked over behind the counter, paper was strewn everywhere, and sawdust had been kicked up onto the shelves.

Ellie looked back at the butcher, who was muttering to himself. "Do you think Mr Frinton is all right?" she whispered to Basil.

Basil glanced over at him. "I'm not sure," he whispered back. "His hat's wonky."

The butcher's hat sat at an angle on his head, and the tassels on the end of his apron were frayed.

As he put the wrapped-up mince down in front of them, he said, "That will be . . . erm . . ." Mr Frinton seemed distracted, but finally told her how much the meat was.

Ellie handed over the money. "Is everything OK?" she asked as she put the packet in her bag.

Mr Frinton gave Ellie her change and sighed. "Not really. A string of sausages was stolen this morning."

"Oh dear!" Ellie exclaimed, looking around the shop. It was clear what had happened. Thieves must have broken in, stolen the sausages and made all this mess. How strange – there was hardly any crime in Greyton . . . unless you included Mr and Mrs Scrudge's criminal cooking!

"Have you called the police?" asked Basil.

"You should," said Ellie, "if you've been burgled—"

But then she stopped because

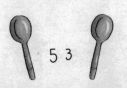

Mr Frinton was laughing. "Oh no, you've misunderstood me! We weren't burgled," he said. "The sausage thief was a little puppy!"

Basil laughed too, but Ellie didn't. Could this little puppy be the same little puppy they were looking for?

"Can you describe him?" she asked.

"He was very playful," Mr Frinton told her, still chuckling. "Wanted to play with the paper. He jumped about in the sawdust, then chewed on the ends of my apron tassels." That

explained the mess in the shop! "I tried to
catch him, but he kept wriggling away."

"What did he look like?" asked Basil.

"He was black with a brown nose. He
had a long body with short legs – and
he had a bright blue ribbon tied
around his neck."

Ellie and Basil looked at
each other. "Abdul's puppy!"
they said together. Whisk
miaowed.

"Did you see where he went?"
asked Ellie.

Mr Frinton smiled. "After he snaffled
the sausages off the counter, he shot out of

the shop door." He pointed up the road in the direction of the village green. "He ran that way."

Ellie didn't waste a second. She ran out of the butcher's and along the high street, with Basil and Whisk just behind her. They called, "Thank you, Mr Frinton!" as they left. And then they were off to track down the playful puppy.

Chapter 5

It was after lunch time when they arrived at the village green. It had been a very busy morning, and they were hungry and a little tired from running. Even Whisk seemed exhausted. But there was no time to eat – they had to find the puppy.

Ahead of them was a wide open space, with some trees with white trunks around

the edge — her dad had once told Ellie that they were silver birch trees. The green was about as big as a football pitch, and over on one side a few children were playing catch. In the far corner a woman was walking her big shaggy sheepdog.

Unfortunately, there was no sign of the puppy.

"What shall we do now?" said Basil.

Ellie wished Victoria Sponge was here: she'd know what to do.

Thinking of Victoria Sponge gave her an idea. "Let's look in my recipe book. Maybe there's a new instruction, now that we've got the minced meat." She really hoped the magic was going to work.

Ellie took the book out of her bag and laid it on the grass. When she turned to the latest recipe — *A perfect pie for a perfect pet* — she saw that she was right. There was a new instruction which hadn't been there before.

5 9

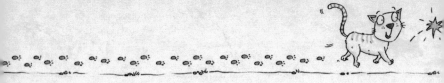

To make the pie you will need a stick.

"A *stick?*" exclaimed Basil, reading over Ellie's shoulder. "Why would anyone add a stick to a meat pie? Who'd want to eat a stick?!"

It did sound rather odd. But then Ellie realized: "It must mean a *cinnamon* stick, to add flavour."

Basil looked relieved. "That makes sense," he said.

When Ellie looked at the book again,

there was a new handwritten note beside
the instruction:

*Find a stick from outside, made from
chewy wood.*

Ellie didn't understand. She'd never
heard of a recipe with actual wood in it!

"Are you sure the book's still working?"
asked Basil.

Ellie put the book back in her bag and
stood up. "Victoria Sponge said we should
follow the recipe exactly, so that's what
we're going to do."

Basil sprang to his feet, and Whisk did

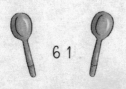

too. They all started looking around on the grass for a stick.

"The best place to find a fallen stick must be near a tree," Ellie suggested.

They walked towards the birch trees on the far side of the green. But they'd taken only a few paces when Ellie stumbled. Her feet were tangled up in something and she fell onto the grass. She chuckled. "The Scrudges are always saying I should look where I'm going. Maybe they're right."

"There's a first time for everything." Basil laughed too as he helped her up.

But then he looked back

at what Ellie had tripped over. "Here's a stick!" he said.

"Well done, Basil!" she said. "I suppose sometimes it pays not to look where you're going!"

Basil laughed again.

"Do you think the stick will be right for our pie?" she asked. "The recipe said it had to be *chewy*."

Basil inspected the stick, which was pale, like the tree trunks. "It's definitely chewy . . ." He showed it to Ellie.

She looked closely. The stick had teeth marks in it; *little* teeth marks.

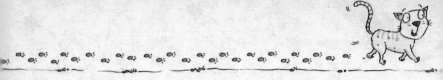

"*Woof, woof!*" came a bark from behind them.

Whisk miaowed and jumped up into Ellie's arms. Ellie turned to see the big sheepdog they'd spotted across the green earlier. His owner, an old woman wearing a purple hat, was right behind him.

"Don't be scared," the woman said. "Biscuit just wants to play with your stick."

Basil stroked the big dog on the head.

"Why is your dog called Biscuit?"

The woman chuckled. "Because biscuits are his favourite food!"

Ellie wanted to give the stick they'd found to Biscuit, but she needed it for their *Perfect pie* recipe. "I'm sorry," she said to the sheepdog. "Shall I find you a different stick to play with?"

The dog woofed, which Ellie took to mean, *Yes please!*

"He was having a tug-of-war with that one a few minutes ago, you see," said the woman.

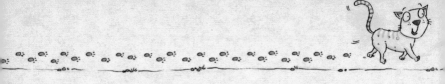

"He was playing with an adorable little puppy wearing a bright blue ribbon."

Ellie and Basil looked at each other and gasped. "Abdul's puppy!"

"Our friend Abdul has lost his puppy, and it sounds like he might have been here. Did you see which way the puppy went?" Ellie asked the woman.

Her face fell. "No, I'm sorry," she said. "Biscuit went chasing after a seagull so I followed him."

"Well, it's good news that the puppy was here," said Ellie.

Basil sighed. "But we're still no closer to finding him."

Basil was right, but they couldn't lose hope now. "Let's go back to the bakery and see if Victoria Sponge has any ideas," suggested Ellie.

Basil nodded.

Ellie grabbed a different stick, much bigger and tougher than the one they'd found, and threw it for Biscuit. Biscuit woofed as he ran after it, his tail wagging.

Then Ellie, Basil and Whisk hurried back to the bakery, taking their smaller, chewy stick with them.

As soon as Ellie entered the bakery she could tell that there was something wrong.

"Do you see that, Basil?" she said.

"See what?"

It didn't look as messy as Scrudge's Bakery, but there was definitely something different about the shop this afternoon. Small differences, like the ones Ellie had noticed in Mr Frinton's shop earlier. Chairs weren't pushed under the tables properly, and there were smudges on the glass of the cake counter. The cake boxes were still stacked in a pyramid, but

68

the pyramid was upside-down and looked ready to topple over!

"I put the CLOSED sign up when we left, but I think someone's been in here," said Ellie.

She walked towards the counter where all the cakes were laid out. Looking closely, she saw that the rock cakes had been swapped with actual rocks!

"There's something wrong with my chocolate doughnuts too," said Basil as he picked one up and inspected it. "These

sprinkles don't look right."

Ellie peered over and realized that the sprinkles were much smaller than the ones they had used. In fact, they didn't look like chocolate at all – they were much darker and *spikier*!

"I think these sprinkles are Mr Scrudge's beard stubble!" exclaimed Ellie. So that's why he had shaved today! *Yuck!*

But her disgust was suddenly replaced by a sense of dread. Where was Victoria Sponge?

"Victoria Sponge!" she cried. "Victoria Sponge!"

Basil joined in too, but for the first time

70

since they'd met her, Victoria Sponge
didn't appear when they called her name.

Then Ellie heard a muffled cry. "Shh!"
she said to Basil. "Listen."

The sound came again. They followed it
into the bakery kitchen. Whisk scampered
over to a cake on the worktop. It was the
gigantic Victoria sponge cake, and the cry
was definitely coming from *inside* it.

Ellie lifted off the top layer of cake to
find Victoria Sponge squashed face
down in the cream and jam.

"Victoria Sponge! Are
you OK?" Ellie helped her
up. "Who did all this?"

71

Victoria scowled, and wiped the jam off her once-white apron. "Who do you think?" she said. "It was those horrible Scrudges! They scooped the cream out of my cake and then squirted in shaving foam. I was secretly trying to fix it when I got squashed inside."

Now Ellie realized why the Scrudges had been waiting outside her bakery earlier, and why they had been so nice to her. They were waiting there to ruin her shop! Mrs Scrudge had said something about Ellie's Magical Bakery being rubbish – and now Ellie knew that the Scrudges planned to ruin it themselves.

Chapter 6

Whisk gave Victoria Sponge a lick, but when he tasted shaving foam instead of cream, he spat it out in disgust.

Victoria Sponge waved her wooden spoon, and the jam on her apron dis-appeared with a puff of glitter. She didn't look dirty any more, but she did look very cross! "Horrible Scrudges," she muttered.

Ellie didn't blame Victoria Sponge for

feeling angry; she felt angry too. "What have they done with all my nice cakes?"

Basil was standing by the bin. He pulled a face. "I think I've found them."

Ellie stomped over and joined him. Peering down, she saw all the delicious biscuits, cakes, doughnuts and rock cakes she and her best friends had been baking all morning. Each one had been crushed and chucked into the bin. They were ruined, and the floor was filthy.

"We don't have any cakes to sell now," said Basil. "We should go over to their bakery and ruin *their* cakes."

"It's tempting," agreed Ellie. "But their cakes are already yucky when they come out of the oven." She tucked her hair behind her ears and took a deep breath – they had bigger problems than ruined cakes! "Oh well," she said. "I was thinking of closing the shop today anyway. Abdul's puppy is still missing and I want to finish the recipe to see if we can find him."

"That's very nice of you, Ellie," said Victoria Sponge.

75

"I hope Abdul would do the same for me if Whisk ever got lost," she said, stroking Whisk on the head.

By the time Ellie looked up, the magical bakery was spotless again. The chairs were pushed in straight, the cake counter was smudge-free, the boxes were piled the right way up, and all the spoiled food had been thrown away. Victoria Sponge must have done it all with magic.

"Thank you," Ellie said to her. "Now we can start preparing the pie."

This time, when Ellie opened the recipe book to the page for *A perfect pie for a perfect pet*, the recipe was frantically writing itself!

76

It gave instructions to fry the meat with some chopped onion and to prepare some savoury shortcrust pastry – enough to line a large pie tin. Then they would spoon the meat mixture carefully into the dish and place a layer of pastry over the top.

They got started straight away!

Ellie put plain flour, butter and a pinch of salt into a bowl. Basil poured in some

water. The dough was so firm they both had to hold the wooden spoon and stir the mixture.

When the pastry was ready, Ellie spread flour over the worktop, and she and Basil rolled it out with a rolling pin. Whisk sneezed as the flour wafted up into the air, but soon the pie tin was lined and ready. Ellie followed the instructions and added the meat filling. Then Victoria Sponge helped her fit the pastry top onto the pie tin, cutting off the extra bits that flopped over the edge. The tiny baker added a final sprinkle of her magical fairy dust, and the pie was ready to bake!

"What does it say to do with the stick?" asked Basil.

Ellie read the instructions.

Serving suggestion: Once the pie is baked, place the stick to one side of it.

That made a bit more sense than putting the stick *in* the pie, but it was still mysterious!

"Why would the recipe ask for the stick?" she wondered.

"I don't know," said Victoria Sponge, "but your father wrote those notes for a reason."

Ellie knew that her father was an excellent baker — could he have used this magical recipe book as well?

"Are you saying my father used this book?" Ellie loved the idea that her dad had followed the instructions, just like she had. As she thought of him, she remembered the aroma of freshly baked cakes. "And is this my father's handwriting?" Ellie asked Victoria Sponge.

"I don't know," she replied

80

– though Ellie saw a twinkle in her eye. Victoria *did* know, she was sure of it. "But chefs often make little notes beside their recipes – like suggestions."

If Ellie's dad had anything to do with the notes in her recipe book, she wanted to follow them exactly.

All they had to do now was put the pie in the oven.

Within minutes the kitchen was filled with the yummy smells of cooking meat and pastry. Whisk miaowed, and sniffed the air. He wanted the first slice!

"It's not for you, I'm afraid,

81

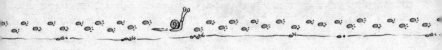

Whisk," Ellie told him with a chuckle.

The three of them stared through the oven window, watching the pie. The pastry turned a lovely golden brown as it cooked! When the timer rang, Victoria Sponge put on some miniature oven gloves, slid the pie out of the oven and placed it carefully on the counter. She really was very strong for such a small person!

Whisk licked his lips.

"What do we do next?" Ellie asked Basil, who was standing closer to the recipe book.

82

Basil squinted down at the recipe. "It says, *Now the pie has to cool. Think of somewhere nice where it can do this.*"

Ellie came over and read it for herself. "I know," she said. "Let's take it to my secret hiding place by the waterfall. Then we can go for a swim while it cools. We might even see Abdul's puppy there. Basil, go and get your swimming shorts, and we'll meet you at the pool."

Basil ran off.

Ellie wasn't sure how making the perfect pie would help her to find Abdul's puppy — she just

hoped the magic of the recipe would work!

Chapter 7

The pool was in a clearing in the nearby wood where a small waterfall trickled down a rocky slope and gathered at the bottom. The water was clean and fresh. Ellie loved swimming there.

She placed the meat pie carefully on a log to cool, and laid the stick down beside it, just as the recipe had suggested. Then Ellie took off her tracksuit, raced to the

side of the pool and dived in.

"Careful!" said Victoria Sponge as she floated above her. "You nearly splashed me!"

Ellie trod water as she watched Whisk scamper off towards the trees. She must have splashed him too. "Sorry, Whisk!" she called after him.

Ellie's swimming costume was black, with a Union Jack on the bottom corner. When Basil arrived, Ellie saw that his swimming shorts had dolphins swimming across them. He jumped into the pool beside her and they both started swimming. Basil splashed a lot but he kept his head above water.

86

"Can you do front crawl, Ellie?" he asked her.

"Yes," she said. "Let me show you."

Ellie pushed off from one end of the pool and started kicking her legs really fast. Her arms whirled like the blades of a helicopter. When she needed to breathe, she turned her head to the side and gulped in air. A second later, she was at the other end! Ellie lifted her goggles and gave Basil a thumbs up.

His mouth had dropped open. "Wowweee, Ellie!" he gasped. "You're so fast."

"Thanks, Basil," she said.

88

"Swimming was something else my dad taught me to do." Ellie remembered going swimming with him. It often made them really hungry, so afterwards they would head home to eat some of the delicious cakes her dad had made in his bakery. Yum!

Ellie realized she was hungry now – neither she nor Basil had eaten anything since breakfast and it was almost tea time!

"You should enter the Olympics!" said Basil.

Ellie laughed. "I'm not *that* fast."

"Yes, you are," said Victoria Sponge. She was not laughing. "Or you could be, with a little training."

"Swimming and baking are my two favourite things, and they remind me of my father," said Ellie. "Speaking of baking . . . Has the pie cooled yet?"

They all looked over at the log.

There was nothing there.

The pie had gone!

Ellie leaped out of the pool and rushed over to where she'd left it. Basil and

Victoria Sponge were right behind her. The dish was still there, but the pie was most definitely not!

There was also someone else who was most definitely not there.

"Whisk!" cried Ellie. "He must have gobbled it up."

She was even more worried about Abdul's lost puppy now. With the pie gone, how could the magic help them find him?

"Whisk!" she called into the trees. "Whisk, come back! I'm not cross with you!"

91

Whisk came padding back through the woods and jumped up onto the log, miaowing.

"Whisk," Ellie said, "you shouldn't run off like that." She picked him up and held him close. "Now, did you eat the pie that we left here?"

She pointed at the empty pie dish, but Whisk just looked at her finger.

"Oh well," she said. "We'll just have to start again, I suppose. Go back to the butcher's and—"

Ellie was interrupted by a loud rumbling from Whisk's tummy. "Oh – Whisk's

hungry!" she cried. "Which means he can't have eaten the pie . . ."

"I'm hungry too," said Basil. Luckily he had brought some sandwiches. He handed one to Ellie and they started to eat.

Ellie sat on the log, took a bite of sandwich and tried to think. "If Whisk

didn't eat the pie, who did?" she wondered aloud.

Victoria Sponge shrugged.

The children finished their sandwiches in silence. Then Ellie noticed that something else was missing. "Hang on . . ." she said. "The stick has gone too!"

"And look what I've found!" Basil was holding a bright blue ribbon.

"Abdul's puppy must have been here! Perhaps he smelled the pie and ate it while we were swimming!" Ellie cried.

"Then took the stick away when he left," said Basil.

The recipe from Ellie's dad *had* worked,

but they had missed the puppy. "We were too busy swimming to see him," said Ellie, feeling annoyed with herself.

She put her cat back down on the ground. "Come on, Whisk," she said. "Help us look."

Ellie wrapped herself in her towel and began searching for the little dog. "Puppy!" she shouted loudly. "Puppy!"

"This would be a lot easier if the dog had a name," said Basil, searching through the bushes.

Victoria Sponge hovered above them. "Can you see anything from up there?" asked Ellie.

"I can see a rabbit and a squirrel, and a sparrow in its nest," she said. "But I can't see the puppy."

They searched and searched the surrounding wood, but there was no sign of him. Ellie had gone around the clearing in a big circle and was back where she'd started. It was hopeless. She sat down on the log and put her head in her hands. "What do we do now?" she wondered.

Basil sat beside her. "Maybe more

96

instructions will appear if we look inside the magical recipe book," he suggested.

It was worth a try. Ellie opened it at the right page – *A perfect pie for a perfect pet.* They waited, but nothing happened. The rest of the pages were blank.

Ellie felt frustrated – she started to cry. "I tried to find Abdul's puppy, and I've failed. I'm trying to run a good little bakery, but the Scrudges want to ruin it."

"You don't need to worry about those horrible Scrudges, Ellie?" Basil, put his arm round her.

97

She sniffed. "Mr and Mrs Scrudge are always calling me stupid. What if it's true?" she asked. "Today I feel stupid."

Basil gave a nice laugh. "Are you kidding, Ellie? You are anything but stupid. You have the yummiest bakery in the village – so yummy that the Scrudges are really jealous. That's why they ruined your cakes! You're a brilliant baker, and you're kind too, helping Abdul look for his puppy. And you are the fastest swimmer I've ever seen!"

Ellie had to smile. She was very lucky to have a friend like Basil. Whisk rubbed up against her legs – his way of comforting

98

her. Ellie felt lucky to have him too.

She looked down at the book again, and was surprised to see another simple handwritten note appear on the blank page.

Be yourself. You are wonderful as you are.

Ellie looked up at Victoria Sponge. The tears in her eyes made the tiny magical baker look extra-specially twinkly.

"Did my dad write that?" she asked her.

Victoria Sponge flew up close to Ellie. "I don't know," she said honestly. "But I do know that he thought you were wonderful."

99

"Cheer up, Ellie," Basil said. "Haven't you ever heard anyone ever say, 'Good things come in small packages'? That's you!"

Ellie laughed.

A brilliant idea had popped into her head.

She jumped up off the log and started running back to the bakery.

"Where are you going?" Basil shouted, chasing after her.

"You were right, Basil," she called back. "Good things do come in small packages. And we're going to use that to find Abdul's puppy!"

Chapter 8

"Free cupcakes!" Ellie shouted. "Come and try a free cupcake!"

The sun was beginning to set as Ellie stood outside her magical bakery with a tray of miniature cupcakes.

A man walked over to her, and when he looked up and smiled, she saw that it was the customer who had come into Scrudge's Bakery yesterday. Ellie remembered that

he had come to Greyton especially to taste the cakes in her shop. Now she had the chance to let him try her baking!

"They look delicious," he said. "May I take one?"

"Please do," said Ellie.

He picked up a cupcake from her tray. It had a sponge base, bright blue icing, and a little bone on top, made out of chocolate. The man took a bite, and an enormous grin

spread across his face. "This is delicious! I'll definitely be back to try more of the treats from *this* bakery."

"But would you please take one of these too?" asked Abdul. He was standing beside Ellie and he handed the man a piece of paper. Ellie had asked Abdul to bring along more of his *LOST PUPPY!* flyers, so they could hand one out with each free cupcake. "If my puppy makes it all the way to your village, please would you let us know? I'm desperate to find him."

The man nodded. "Of course I will. And I'll stick this flyer up in my window, so my neighbours can read it too. Someone must

have spotted him!" He smiled again, thanked Ellie for the cupcake, and walked away with Abdul's flyer in his hand.

Ellie's Magical Bakery had been closed all day, and it was never usually open this late, but the children wanted to find the missing puppy before it got dark. Ellie's idea was that giving away small but delicious cakes for free would attract attention, and help them find out if anyone had seen Abdul's puppy. And the more flyers they gave out, the better

chance they had of finding him quickly.

Basil was right: good things *did* come in small packages – just like these little cupcakes. And just like Ellie.

"Thank you for doing this for me, Ellie," said Abdul.

Basil, on his roller skates, brought Mr Amrit and Mr Frinton with him towards the shop. "I've told everyone I've seen," he called. "They're all coming over to try your cupcakes and take a flyer!"

It was lucky that Ellie and Victoria Sponge had made so many! As the cakes were so small, they hadn't taken too long to bake.

"When I heard you were giving out free cake, I had to shut my shop early," said Mr Frinton, taking a cupcake from Ellie's tray. "Ellie's Magical Bakery is the best bakery I have ever been to."

"Ellie's an amazing baker," said Basil. "And she's just as good at swimming."

Ellie was beaming with pride. Then she remembered something she wanted to tell Basil. She'd come up with another idea after they went swimming. "I have

decided what I want to do with the money I make from the bakery."

"Oh, really?" said Basil. "What's that?"

"I'm going to save up enough money to go to the Olympic Park in London and swim in the pool there. I want to swim at the Olympics one day!"

Basil clapped his hands. "That's a great idea, Ellie! I know you'll make it."

"There's no reason why I can't," she replied, thinking of her

dad's note in her recipe book. *Be yourself.*

Out of the corner of her eye, Ellie saw Colin Scrudge across the road. He was laughing at her. "A shrimp like *you*? In the Olympics?"

Ellie took a deep breath, and tried not to be upset by his sneering. "What do you want, Colin?"

"Shrimpy cakes, made by a shrimp," he said, strolling over to her. "I bet they're disgusting."

"You won't want one, then, will you?" Ellie replied.

Colin's face fell and he reached for a cupcake. "Maybe just one," he said. "Just

to test exactly how disgusting they are."

Ellie rolled her eyes and let him take one. She knew it wasn't about beating the bullies – she just had to be herself.

Then came a familiar sound. "*Woof, woof!*"

There was the shaggy sheepdog Ellie had met earlier, with his owner, the lady with the purple hat. Basil led them over to Ellie and Abdul.

"Abdul," he said, "this lady saw your puppy today."

Abdul's eyes lit up. "Really? Was he OK?"

The woman smiled. "He was more than OK. He was playing with my dog, Biscuit."

Abdul smiled sadly. "He is a very playful puppy."

The woman took a cupcake from Ellie's tray. Before she popped it into her mouth she asked, "What did you use that stick for? I saw bits of it all the way up the high street."

Ellie gasped. She looked at Abdul and then at Basil. Both of them were wide-

eyed and hopeful. Could it be a trail to
the lost puppy?

"What are we waiting for?" cried Ellie.

"Here!" said Mr Frinton. "Take this."

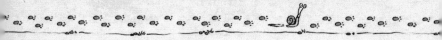

He handed Basil a string of sausages. "The pup's favourite food might help to lure him out of hiding!"

Ellie, Basil, Abdul and Whisk started up the high street. It wasn't long before they found what they were looking for – a chewed-up bit of bark. It was the same whitish colour as the silver birch trees on the green. "It has to be the stick we found!" said Basil.

There were more and more bits of wood trailing up the high street. Eventually the debris led into the last place Ellie would have expected – Scrudge's Bakery.

Inside, Mrs Scrudge was slumped in her

usual place behind the till. She sneered at Ellie and her friends as they came in. "Given up on your rubbish bakery, have you?"

Mr Scrudge came out of the kitchen. "I heard you had beard-hair in your food," he said with a laugh. "How disgusting!"

"You are too small and stupid to run a bakery – we told you before," added Mrs Scrudge. "Now do you believe us?"

Basil and Abdul stood beside Ellie, and Ellie stood up tall. "I may be small, but even *I* would have to get down very low to stoop to your level."

"I'll show you!" said Mr Scrudge, and he

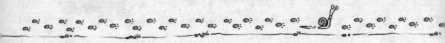

made a swipe to grab Ellie. But Ellie and her friends stepped back and Mr Scrudge slipped. He fell flat on his bottom.

Mrs Scrudge jumped up to catch him, but she slipped too – landing on top of him.

Basil covered his mouth, trying not to laugh.

"What was that?" Mr Scrudge howled at the pile of something he had slipped on.

Ellie didn't know, but it looked – and smelled! – like something a puppy

might have left behind . . .

She didn't wait to find out, as she and the others raced upstairs to the flat.

"Puppy!" Abdul cried. "Come here, puppy!"

Ellie saw a piece of stick just outside her bedroom door. Could the puppy really be hiding in there? They all crept inside.

Ellie's bedroom looked neat and tidy as usual, but they started to search for clues.

She checked under her bed while Abdul opened a cupboard and Basil searched behind the

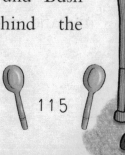

curtain. Whisk miaowed loudly, which was his way of helping.

While Abdul's back was turned, Ellie opened the magical recipe book to let out Victoria Sponge.

"We've followed the trail all the way here," Ellie whispered to her. "We still can't find the puppy, though. Now what do we do?"

"Try waving the sausages around," suggested Victoria Sponge, then tucked herself away into the collar of Ellie's top.

Ellie closed the book and did as Victoria had

116

suggested. She waved the sausages around, hoping the puppy would pick up on the scent.

Whisk miaowed loudly again.

"Thanks for your help, Whisk, but—" Ellie gasped when she saw what Whisk was miaowing at.

There was Abdul's puppy! He was fast asleep in Whisk's cat bed, with the remains of a very chewed stick poking out of his mouth.

The puppy woke up and Whisk nuzzled his ears.

"Abdul! Look!"

The little boy ran over and gathered up the puppy in his arms.

"He must have been tired after all his adventures," Basil realized.

The puppy gave Abdul a big lick on the cheek – he was as happy to see Abdul as Abdul was to see him. "Thanks so much for helping me find him, both of you," said Abdul.

Whisk miaowed.

"Sorry, Whisk! And you too!"

"I bet he's hungry," Abdul said. "He's had a big day!"

"Here," said Basil as he handed a sausage to the little dog. "The butcher reckons they're his favourite."

"*That's* what you should call him!" cried Ellie. "Why don't you name him after his favourite food? Just like that dog Biscuit. He could be Sausage the sausage dog who loves sausages!"

Abdul laughed and hugged his puppy tightly. "It's the perfect name for a perfect pet."

Victoria Sponge popped out of Ellie's

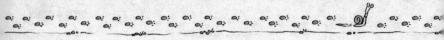

collar and whispered into her ear, "Well done, Ellie. Now why don't you invite Basil and Abdul back to the bakery for some cake? I bet Sausage isn't the only one who's hungry!"

Whisk looked hungrily up at them.

Ellie thought it was a great idea too. It had been a very busy, very strange day. But at last they'd found Abdul's new puppy, Sausage, which was an absolutely perfect ending.

Hello, lovely to see you!

Do you like to bake?

Why don't you try out Ellie's recipe?

Make sure you always have
a grown-up around to help.

When the cupcakes are ready,
why don't you invite some friends over
to share them with you?

Happy Baking!

Victoria Sponge

Mini Cupcakes
with Blue Icing and
Chocolate Decoration

Ingredients:

110g/4oz butter or margarine,
softened at room temperature

110g/4oz caster sugar

2 free-range eggs, lightly beaten

1 tsp vanilla extract

110g/4oz self-raising flour

1-2 tbsp milk

20g cocoa powder

For the buttercream icing:

140g/5oz butter, softened

280g/10oz icing sugar

1-2 tbsp milk

a few drops of blue food colouring

Cake Recipe

1. Preheat the oven to 180C and line a 12-hole muffin tin with paper cases.

2. Cream the butter and sugar together in a bowl until pale. Beat in the eggs a little at a time and stir in the vanilla extract.

3. Fold in the flour and cocoa powder using a large metal spoon, adding a little milk until the mixture. Spoon the mixture into the paper cases until they are half full.

4. Bake in the oven for 10-15 minutes, or until golden-brown on top and a skewer inserted into one of the cakes comes out clean. Set aside to cool for 10 minutes, then remove from the tin and cool on a wire rack.

Icing Recipe

5. For the buttercream icing, beat the butter in a large bowl until soft. Add half the icing sugar and beat until smooth.

6. Then add the remaining icing sugar with one tablespoon of the milk, adding more milk if necessary, until the mixture is smooth and creamy.

7. Add the food colouring and mix until well combined.

8. Spoon the icing into a piping bag with a star nozzle and pipe the icing.

Chocolate Decoration Recipe:

1. Melt some chocolate in the glass bowl over a pan of simmering water until smooth.

2. Make a small piping bag out of baking parchment or use a shop-bought piping bag.

3. Half-fill the piping bag with the melted chocolate and pipe out a design of your choice on to a sheet of baking paper. You could make mini chocolate dog bones like Ellie, or anything you like such as stars or flowers.

4. Set the chocolate aside in a cool place to set fully.

5. Carefully peel the chocolate decorations off from the sheet and place on top of the cupcakes.

Read on for
a sneak peek of
Ellie's first
baking adventure!

Ellie's Magical Bakery

Best Cake for a Best Friend

♥ ELLIE SIMMONDS ♥

Illustrated by Kimberley Scott

RED FOX

Chapter 1

It was the morning of Ellie's birthday. Before she stepped into Scrudge's Bakery she took a deep breath to give herself courage . . . then wished she hadn't. The bakery smelled like old socks and soggy cabbage. *Revolting, as usual*, Ellie thought.

She looked around the bakery, hoping she might have a birthday present. The shelves were lined with week-old bread,

stale, stodgy cakes and mouldy muffins. Her uncle, Mr Scrudge, stood behind one of the shop counters mixing cookie dough. Ellie watched as he shoved a fistful of chocolate chips into his mouth, then swept a handful of dead flies off the worktop and into the dough. *Yuck!*

And there was no sign of a present.

Ellie knew very little about her mum, and her dad had died three years ago. She remembered his ginger beard, round cheeks and silly deep chuckle. Whenever she thought about him she was surrounded by the aroma of freshly baked cakes . . . not this horrible smell! Her aunt and uncle ran her father's bakery now.

They had changed the name of the shop to 'Scrudge's Bakery' and had moved into the flat above it with Ellie and her ginger cat, Whisk.

She hadn't had a birthday present since.

Mrs Scrudge was slouching in a chair behind the till, her belly squeezing out of the top of her trousers. "What do *you* want, Shrimp?" she asked Ellie, straining to reach a mug of tea.

Ellie passed her the mug. There *was* something she wanted – even more than a present. She was going

138

to ask her aunt and uncle
for a special birthday treat.

Whisk ran over and
rubbed up against her leg.
It gave her courage.

"Umm, it's my birth—"
she started to say.

But the door to the shop suddenly
opened and a man walked in.

"Customers! Quiet!" hissed Mrs Scrudge,
and heaved herself up in her chair.

Whisk hissed. Ellie stroked his fur and
looked up to see who it was. Customers
were rare since the Scrudges had taken
over the bakery. It was Mr Amrit,

a man she'd seen around the village. Clearly he hadn't heard how awful the food was here.

He strode up to the counter confidently, then caught sight of the horrible-looking cakes, cringed, and held his nose.

"Hello, sir," Mrs Scrudge simpered, batting her eyelashes. "Do buy something from our delightful shop."

"Er . . . no thank you," said Mr Amrit, backing out of the door. "I've just remembered, I . . ."

Ellie went to hold the door for him – she couldn't blame Mr Amrit for wanting to leave. But her aunt lunged forward

and grabbed Ellie's arm while her uncle blocked poor Mr Amrit's exit. Mr Scrudge was huge – the size of a garden shed – with stubble on his face and neck.

"Buy something from our delightful shop," he growled. "Or else!" He put up his fist.

Mr Amrit cowered, then forced a smile onto his face. "My wife *is* partial to carrot cake," he said, his voice shaking with fear. "D–d–do you have some?"

Mrs Scrudge gave him a slice of cake. It was furrier than Whisk.

"Do you think that's safe to eat?" Ellie asked her aunt. "It looks a bit green."

"'Course it's green," Mrs Scrudge snapped.

"It's Brussels sprout cake."

Ellie winced.

Mr Amrit winced.

Even Whisk winced.

Who would want to eat a Brussels sprout cake?

"It was *carrot* cake I was after," Mr Amrit said. "You know, with the creamy white icing—'

Mr Scrudge raised his fists again and Mr Amrit said, "But this looks nice too." He took the cake, handed over his money and hurried out of the shop.

"Come back soon!" called Mrs Scrudge, then she slumped back in her chair, puffing from the effort.

Ellie felt terribly sorry for Mr Amrit. Cakes were supposed to be delicious, tasty treats. The Scrudges' definitely weren't.

She'd never dared eat any of their cakes — not since she'd heard worrying gurgly noises coming from the tummies of the villagers who had. But when Ellie was younger, her dad had let her help in the bakery. She wanted to try baking again — to make her very own birthday cake.

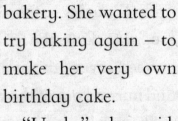

"Uncle," she said. "It's my birth—"

"I'm busy!" he yelled at her. But he was only busy cleaning out his ears with his finger.

"I could help you in the bakery if you like." Ellie pulled her long brown hair into a ponytail, ready to get stuck in.

Mr Scrudge turned and laughed. "Don't be ridiculous!"

Mrs Scrudge laughed too. "You are too small and too stupid to make cakes. In fact, you're too small and too stupid to do anything."

Ellie crossed her arms in front of her chest. She *was* small. She had a condition called achondroplasia, which meant she was shorter than most people.

But there was no such thing as *too small*. An ant can lift things fifty times heavier than itself. A salmon swims thousands of miles. Even the smallest birthday present can make a person very happy.

And Ellie was most certainly *not* stupid.

"But if you would like to prove you're not completely useless," Mrs Scrudge said, "go to the garden centre and get me some cement mix. I can't be bothered."

"Why do you need cement mix?" Ellie asked.

"It's cheaper than flour," her aunt replied.

"And mud is cheaper than chocolate," added Mr Scrudge.

Yuck!

"Can't Colin go?" Ellie asked. Colin was her cousin, the Scrudges' twelve-year-old son.

"No," said Mrs Scrudge. "He's out."

Ellie was certain Colin *was* out: he was

probably out bullying someone.

"Fine," she said. It was annoying how lazy the Scrudges were, but she was pleased to have an excuse to get away from them.

"Make sure you're back by four," Mr Scrudge called after her. "Or I'll put Whiskers in the next batch!" He threw a burned bun at Ellie's cat.

Whisk miaowed, annoyed.

Ellie snapped back, "My cat's name is *Whisk*!"

"What's a whisk?" said Mrs Scrudge.

Ellie shook her head in dismay – any baker should know what a whisk was!

She held the door open for the cat as they left the shop.

Then she stumbled.

At first she assumed that Colin had left something on the ground on purpose, to trip her up; he'd done that before. But when she looked down, she gasped with surprise. There on the doorstep lay a neatly wrapped present about the size of a pizza box. It had a bow on it, the paper was covered in pictures of cupcakes with candles on, and the words *Happy Birthday Ellie* were written on the front.

"Do you think the Scrudges have bought me a birthday present after all?" Ellie wondered aloud. But deep down she knew that there was more chance of Whisk buying her a present than Mr and Mrs Scrudge.

There was a note on the front that said:

Open in secret

Ellie knew just the place . . .

ELLIE SIMMONDS is a Paralympic swimming champion and has ten world records to her name. At 14, Ellie was the youngest recipient of the MBE, and also now has an OBE – both special titles awarded by the Queen. Ellie has continued to succeed in swimming, but she also loves to bake! Working on Ellie's Magical Bakery is a really exciting new way for Ellie to pursue her love of cakes and bakes.

Ellie's disability is called Achondroplasia (dwarfism). Achondroplasia means that Ellie has shorter arms and legs than most people. As a result Ellie is a lot smaller than other people her age, but this has never stopped her from doing the things she loves the most.

KIMBERLEY SCOTT is a professional illustrator and designer. She regularly works on a diverse range of projects and loves to delve into imaginative worlds. Kimberley lives and works in London, from her teeny-weeny studio, with a constant supply of green tea and pick-and-mix sweets to keep her creativity flowing!